A special thanks to my family for their lo

To all the children I have taught over the years,
always remember:

"Use your imagination every day!"

Cookie's Caravan Holiday

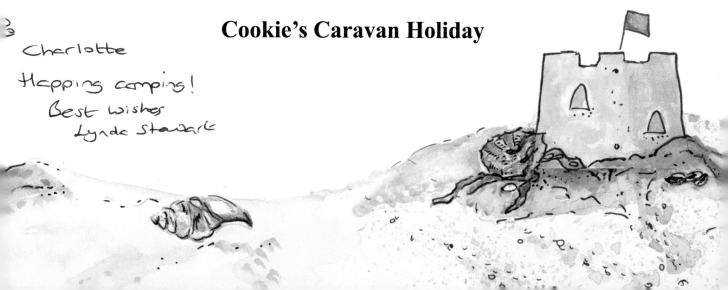

Cookie's Caravan Holiday

It was the first week of the summer holidays, and instead of sunshine…it was pouring with rain!

Huge raindrops, pitter pattered against Cookie's hutch. They trickled down the side and made a big, round, puddle on the ground.

Pitter, Patter, Pitter, Patter! … Drip, Drip Drip!

Cookie looked out onto the dreary garden and saw her friend Sammy snail, moving ever….so…. slowly…. towards her.

"Hello Sammy, where are you going on this rainy day?"

"I'm off on holiday to find some sunshine ….and if it carries on raining, I'll just snuggle back inside my shell house again."

"What a good way of keeping dry," said Cookie.

"Yes, it's nice and cosy in here," replied the snail, and he turned towards the garden shed.

"I hope you have a lovely holiday!" called Cookie and she watched the snail slide away. "I wish I could go on holiday," thought Cookie as she sat inside her damp hutch, listening to the rain.

Pitter, Patter, Pitter, Patter! … Drip, Drip Drip!

The next day, the weather was much better, and the sun was shining.

Cookie nibbled some hay and watched her owners carrying lots of bags into the car.

Then she saw a rectangle shaped house, with windows and a door!......

And it was on wheels!

Cookie was very puzzled. "I wonder what **THAT** is?"

Then her owner opened the hutch and put some spinach into her red bowl.

"Morning Cookie. We're going on holiday today, in a caravan…… to the seaside……and you're coming with us!"

"Ooooh!... a caravan. Ooooh! the seaside," thought Cookie excitedly. "I've never been in a house on wheels before."

A few hours later, everything was ready. The caravan was attached to the back of the car and Cookie placed safely, in her travel cage.

"This reminds me of Sammy's shell house," thought Cookie, and they set off on their journey.

It was a bit bumpy at first, but Cookie didn't mind.

They drove past a stall selling lots of vegetables…carrots, cabbage, and cucumber.

"Umm, I hungry, I hope we're stopping here," thought Cookie, but no - they carried on driving.

Then they went past a field full of hay.

"Umm, I'm still hungry, I hope we're stopping here,"

but no - they carried on driving.

Round and round the bends, up and down the hills and along the country lanes.

Eventually, they drove down a track which led to the campsite. Lots of other families were on holiday too. Cookie saw big caravans and small caravans and colourful tents, all shapes and sizes – and they were all set up around the field.

In the distance, she could see a sandy beach, the sea, and a lighthouse.

She gave out, a long and happy, "**SSSSqqqueeeeaaakkkk!** ….

This is going to be a wonderful holiday," she thought.

Her owners hooked up the caravan and placed Cookie outside, in her cage, under the shade of a big oak tree.

The bags where unpacked and her owners went down to the beach to explore.

From her cage, she could see lots of children on the field, playing football and hide and seek. Some were looking for mini beasts and others climbing trees and riding bicycles.

Everyone was happy.

For the next few days, she enjoyed relaxing, eating and sleeping. They were on holiday for a whole week and each day her owners did something new.

On Monday, the family went swimming in the sea and had donkey rides along the shore.

On Tuesday, they watched a clever man, making sandcastle sculptures of animal shapes on the beach.

On Wednesday, they had so much fun bouncing up and down on the trampolines. Then back at the campsite, the children dressed up as pirates and pretended to look for hidden gold and treasure. There was always lots to do.

On Thursday morning, Cookie's owners had packed another picnic, ready for the beach and were about to leave. They put Cookie in the shade, with lots of food and water as usual.......
BUT.... they didn't realise that they had left her cage door unlocked.
Cookie smiled to herself and thought, "Now it's time for my adventure!"

She nudged the cage door open with her nose, tip toed out onto the field and quickly scurried down the pathway to the beach, before anyone could see her.

The sand felt warm and tickly in-between her guinea pig toes and she ran towards the sea, splashing about in the gentle waves.

First, she walked carefully around the rocks and up towards the lighthouse.
Up and up around the spiral steps until she reached the top.

She looked out to the sea.

When she came back down again, she felt a little bit dizzy and decided to paddle her feet, in the cool water of a rock pool.

Nearby she noticed, a large hermit crab with a shell house on his back. Behind him there were four other smaller hermit crabs, all in a row. One behind the other, behind the other, behind the other. They looked like they were waiting for something.

"Hello," said Cookie. "Why are you all waiting in a queue?"

The biggest hermit crab, called Kevin replied,

"I've grown too big for my shell house now,

so I'm moving out and going into this larger one.

The other hermit crabs are waiting for me to climb out.

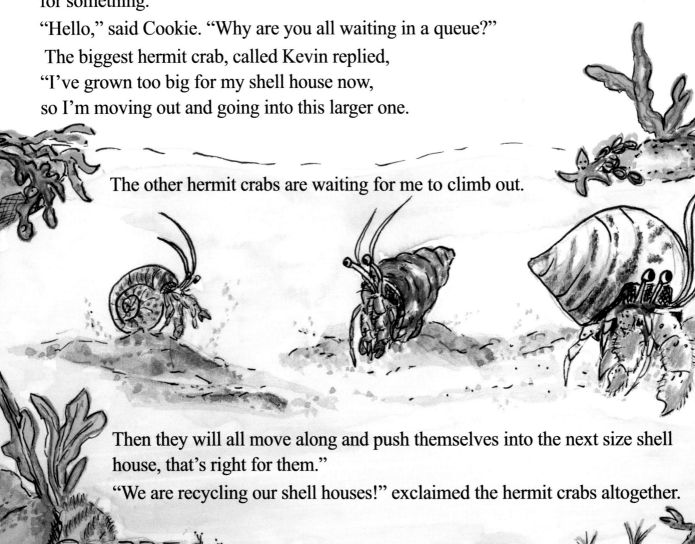

Then they will all move along and push themselves into the next size shell house, that's right for them."

"We are recycling our shell houses!" exclaimed the hermit crabs altogether.

Cookie then watched each hermit crab squirm and wriggle about in the sandy sea water.

Wriggle, Wriggle, Wriggle! ... Push, Push, Push!
Wriggle, Wriggle, Wriggle! ... Push, Push, Push!

Until they were all safely inside their new shell homes.

"Recycling your shell homes is a very clever idea," said Cookie.

"I'm on holiday in a mobile home. It's called a caravan!" she said proudly.

"Yes, just like us. Your house moves around with you too," agreed Kevin.

Enjoy your holiday Cookie!

Then they crawled away to settle into their new shell homes.

Next, Cookie walked back to the beach and found a bucket and spade. She decided to make some sandcastles. She added shells, then a little flag and dug so many holes, that the sand sprinkled all over her whiskers.

"I've had such a busy day, I'm ready for some food and a rest now.... and I want to get back inside my cage before my owners have noticed I've escaped!" thought Cookie.

She followed the path back up to the campsite and stopped to rest near a bench. Her favourite dandelion leaves were growing nearby, and she started to eat.

Munch, Munch, Munch! ... Nibble, Nibble, Nibble!
Munch, Munch, Munch! ... Nibble, Nibble, Nibble!

Two children were sitting there as well, eating the most enormous ice-creams. Creamy, delicious, vanilla ice cream cones with chocolate flakes on top and swirls of raspberry flavoured juice all over them.... but they were beginning to melt in the hot sunshine and trickles of ice cream and raspberry juice, were landing on the grass, right by Cookie!

Trickle, Trickle, Trickle! .... Drip, Drip, Drip!
Trickle, Trickle, Trickle! .... Drip, Drip, Drip!

Cookie noticed and tried to move out of the way, but suddenly,
the whole ice cream cone, slipped out of the girl's hand......
and landed on Cookie's back...... "Splat!"
"Oh Yuk!" squealed Cookie and she quickly ran back
to the caravan, to try and get clean.

By the time she got back, pieces of grass, petals and meadow hay had stuck onto her fur, and she looked more like a flowery hedgehog, than a guinea pig. She tried to pick it off but couldn't reach.

"What have you been doing Cookie?"

asked her owners when they got back from the beach.

They giggled and said,

"Your fur is covered with bits,

and you smell like Cookies and Cream!"

They had no idea where she had been all day.

But as they cleaned and brushed her fur, they found some:

Seaweed ......a paper flag.... a bit of sticky ice cream cone, with dried raspberry juice....and a shell. ......And stuck inside the shell, was a small GOLD coin!

"Look! Cookie....You've found some pirate treasure!

Cookie was shocked......she didn't know how the gold coin had got there.

Her owners put the gold coin and shell, safely in a box and gave Cookie another good clean. They picked her up carefully and went to tell the people at the campsite, what had happened and asked if they knew anything about the gold coin.

seaweed

a paper flag

a shell with a
golden coin inside

ice cream cone

They found out that many years ago, there had been a shipwreck.
All the treasure and gold coins had sunk to the bottom of the sea.
Over the years, pieces of jewellery and coins had been discovered
on the seabed and some were swept up on to the shore.
Cookie had been very lucky to find the gold coin.

After a few days, the gold coin and shell, were taken to a nearby museum and stored safely in a glass display case. Cookie's photo was taken, and the story of the gold coin stuck inside the shell, or "Shelley's Gold," was printed in the local newspaper in Duckleberry Bay.

LOCAL DAILY NEWS AT
DUCKLEBERRY BAY

Cookie, the guinea pig finds gold coin in shell!

The gold coin is part of the treasure from a shipwreck from one hundred years ago! It is not known how the gold coin became stuck in Cookie's fur, but the blob of ice cream seemed to help. Her owners cleaned her and found the gold coin stuck inside a shell. It is now on display in Duckleberry Bay Museum and is called, "Shelly's Gold!" Cookie was asked to comment and replied with a "Sssquuueeeaaaakkkk!"

Cookie was now famous!

They all shouted,
"Hip Hip Hooray for Cookie!"
and gave her a special certificate
and some extra carrots to eat.

She was so happy.
Cookie had been to the seaside,
had stayed in a caravan.... and
had found some treasure......
it really had been, the best
holiday ever!

The time had come to pack everything away into the caravan and the family got back into the car, just as it started to rain again.

"I wonder if Sammy snail has had as much fun as me, on his holiday?" thought Cookie dreamily. Then she snuggled down in her hay and nodded off to sleep, listening to the sound of the rain, pitter pattering against the windows.

Pitter, Patter, Pitter, Patter! .... Drip, Drip, Drip!

Sammy Snail

Cookie in her hutch.

The gold coin & shells.

Facts About Garden Snails

Garden snails like to live in dark, damp parts of the garden. They eat leaves, fruits, vegetables and decomposing organic matter. They have 14,000 teeth arranged in rows on their tongue.

They move very slowly and leave a sticky, slime trail behind them.

Snails lay tiny, white eggs in the soil and after around 21 days, little baby snails hatch out.

As the snail grows bigger, their protective shell grows bigger with them. By counting their growth rings, you can guess their age.

Facts About Hermit Crabs

Hermit crabs live in large colonies of 100 or more and can be found near rocky shores and on the seabed.

They have a soft, hook shaped body and 5 pairs of legs, including a pair of tough pincers. But they cannot grow their own shell! They begin by finding a small, empty shell to live in.

As they grow bigger, they search around to find a larger, more protective and suitable shell. The hook shaped body and strong back legs, hold onto the inside of the shell, until it's time to swap over and recycle their shells!

Hermit crabs use their pincers to shred and eat decaying sea creatures, such as squid, fish and other crabs.